THE GREEDY LITTLE COBBLER

PIASTER AZTECA SOU YEN GROSCHEN PAI STIVER
CENTIME FRANC CENT CENTAVO FRANC DOLLAR DRAC
AZTECA ANNA POUND ESCUDO SEN PENNY KOPECK BELGA
GUILDER KOPECK PIASTER SOL DO RIAL SOLDO SEN CONT
PESO SOU FRANC LIRA RUBLE RUPEE SOLDO CENT
RUBLE CONTO YEN PESETA CONTO SHEKEL BELGA
CONTO KRONA PIE DOLLAR REIS CENTAVO
ESCUDO GUILDER DRACHMA DINAR SCHILLING KOPECK ESCU
PESETA STIVER CONTO
SEN BELGA KOPECK KRONA KRONA
KRONA KOPECK LIRA CENT PESO LIRA
CENTIME PAI DOLLAR LIRA KRONA CENTIMO FRANC RIAL CENT
SHEKEL PENNY CENT KRONE BELGA PFEN KRONE DUIT KRONE
CENTIMO PIASTER PIASTER ESCUDO SEN RUBLE
FRANC PESO SCHILLING MARK ESCUDO CENT
AZTECA BELGA CENTAVO RUPEE
FLORIN GULDEN CENTISIMO SHEKEL POUND DOLLAR
SEN SOU RUPEE PFENNIG KOPECK FRANC SHEKEL SOU
PIASTER CENTAVO CONTO RUPEE POUND MARK
REIS DRACHMA SOLDO STIVER
CENTIME STIVER KRONA MARK POUND
SEN CENT PESO DINAR ANNA
MARK CENTIME RIAL FLORIN
SEN STIVER DOLLAR AZTECA YEN SEN
GROSCHEN CENTIMO PESETA CENTISIMO SOLDO ANNA
PESETA DRACHMA RUPEE AZTECA
PESO BELGA DINAR PESO SOU DINAR CENTIM
ALEX GROSCHEN
RUPEE SEN FRANC SEN FRANC RUBLE SCHILLING
PENNY PIASTER CONTO SEN DOLLAR LIRA BELGA POUND

SOL DO CENT DINAR MARK SCHILLING PAI SOU REIS
AZTECA SHEKEL PIASTER PENNY GROSCHEN DINAR YEN ANNA
ESCUDO CONTO MARK PFENNIG SCHILLING CENT STIVER
YEN SOU FLORIN AZTECA RUBLE SEN
PAI FLORIN SCHILLING
GUILDER ESCUDO CENT ANNA MARK FRANC BELGA
YEN CENTESIMO DINAR SOU LIRA
RUBLE REIS BELGA SOU PESETA RUBLE PESETA ESCUDO
ANNA FRANC LIRA DRACHMA YEN SHEKEL
CENTAVO DRACHMA RUBLE KOPECK MARK GROSCHEN PIASTER RUBLE
SOLDO CONTO RUPEE RUPEE LIRA CENTAVO
ESCUDO ANNA REIS KOPECK PENNY KRONA
SOU CONTO SEN CONTO DRACHMA KOPECK SOU
FLORIN STIVER CENTAVO PAI PESETA PIASTER
STIVER REIS CENTIMO PESO SCHILLING REIS STIVER GULDEN
DOLLAR LIRA CENTESIMO KRONA DOLLAR RIAL CENTIME DINAR
SOU PENNY FRANC POUND SHEKEL
PAI PESO GUILDER GROSCHEN FLORIN
KRONE GUILDER LIRA KRONA POUND CENTESIMO FLORIN
SOU KRONE SOLDO AZTECA PENNY RUBLE DOLLAR
POUND ANNA CENTESIMO STIVER KOPECK
PESETA MARK GROSCHEN PESO FRANC SCHILLING
CENTESIMO SOU CENTAVO SHEKEL PESO
BELGA DUIT KOPECK KRONA REIS CENTIMO MARK AZTECA
SCHILLING FLORIN GROSHEN ESCUDO POUND FLORIN
STIVER SOU KRONA DUIT CENT
PIASTER ANNA GUILDER YEN ANNA MARK
GROSCHEN BELGA FRANC SHEKEL
KRONA YEN RUBLE DRACHMA DOLLAR
MARK SEN ESCUDO RIAL
SHEKEL POUND KOPECK
SOL
ESCUDO LIRA PESETA RUBLE

A Beaver Book
Published by Arrow Books Limited
62-5 Chandos Place, London WC2N 4NW
An imprint of Century Hutchinson Ltd

London Melbourne Sydney Auckland
Johannesburg and agencies throughout the world

First published by Andersen Press 1979

Beaver edition 1988

Printed in Italy by Grafiche AZ, Verona

ISBN 0 09 964260 3

THE GREEDY LITTLE COBBLER

by Tony Ross

Beaver Books

Long ago, a little cobbler lived in a little town.
Everybody in the town loved the cobbler and day after day, he would sit at his last mending their shoes.
Nobody had much money, so sometimes the cobbler would take a pig in payment for a pair of shoes, or an egg for a new heel.
Of course, the little cobbler wasn't rich, but he had lots of eggs and bacon for his supper.

Sometimes the little cobbler would make a new pair of shoes for the farmer, and in return would get a load of leather. Or he might put new soles on the blacksmith's boots, and the blacksmith would give him nails, or sharpen his tools. That's what life was like in the little town, with everybody helping everybody else.
In the evenings the cobbler would sit with his good friends and think, "Life's not bad!"

One day, the little cobbler was passing a rich man's house, when he happened to peep over the hedge. The rich man's friends were playing about in the garden.
"Hmm," muttered the cobbler, "my life may be good, but it certainly looks better to be rich!" There and then, the greedy little man decided to mend only the finest shoes. He would ask for LOTS of money in return, and accept no more pigs and eggs.

As the fine lords would not come to the cobbler, he had to go to them. He built himself a little cart and loaded his cobbler's things onto it.
A poor shepherd came to him, asking for a new boot in exchange for a lamb.
"On your way," laughed the cobbler. "I've better boots to mend now!"
At the first great house the cobbler visited, the servants set the dogs on him.
"Not a good start!" gasped the cobbler, scrambling to safety on his cart.

Next, the little cobbler visited the richest lord in the land. He found him in the garden, playing with his falcon.
It happened that the lord's shoes were wearing thin, so the cobbler put on new soles and heels. The work done, he asked for a silver shilling.
"Away with you, sir!" snapped the lord. "I *never* pay tradesmen, it's an honor to work for me. Why, when it becomes known you mend *my* shoes, you'll get all the work you want!"

"Jolly nice of the lord to let me mend his shoes free!" muttered the cobbler as he trudged off towards the colonel's house.
The colonel wanted a new pair of red boots, to wear with his new blue uniform.
The cobbler made the boots from the finest leather.
Putting them on, the colonel leaped on his horse.
"The war's just started!" he yelled, galloping off into the night.
Of course, the colonel had forgotten to pay the cobbler.

As the admiral was in port, the cobbler paid him a visit.
"NEW SEABOOTS, THAT'S THE THING!" boomed the admiral.
The seaboots took a week to make, and they were the most handsome, and the most waterproof boots on the sea.
The admiral was delighted. So delighted, in fact, he sailed away without even remembering to pay the little cobbler.

"Never mind," thought the cobbler, "I now have lots of rich customers. One day I *must* be rich too!"
He made a pair of ballet shoes for the most famous ballerina in the world. They were silver, with pink ribbons and hard toes.
The ballerina was overjoyed.
"They're so comfy," she trilled. "I must dance right away!"
And she did! She danced in the theater that evening, watched by the little cobbler. He hoped she would remember to pay for the shoes after the performance. But when the curtain came down, he never saw her again.

That evening the little cobbler sat all alone in his little shop. Not one of his fine customers had given him a penny, and by this time he had no leather or nails left.
He had no food, or money to buy any, so he was trying to fry an old boot for his supper.
"Oh dear," he wailed, "getting rich has only made me poor."
He just sat there and sobbed.
One by one, his old friends gathered by the window to see what all the noise was about.
"And my feet hurt!" howled the greedy little cobbler.

“No wonder!” cried his old friends, pointing to the floor.
“Look at your shoes!”
The cobbler looked. His shoes were in tatters, quite worn away with pushing his cart from house to house.
It was too much; the cobbler collapsed again in tears.
“I’d still like you to make me a new boot in exchange for the lamb,” said the shepherd shyly. “That is, if you’ve nothing better to do.”
The cobbler dried his eyes, and beamed.
“There’s nothing better than working for old friends,” he said.

In no time at all, the little cobbler had a HUGE pile of shoes to mend.
Of course, he was still paid with pigs and eggs, or sometimes a goose or a hen. But now it didn't seem to matter, as he felt richer than he'd ever felt before. He had plenty to eat again, lots of leather and nails, and more important, he had all his old friends.
Amid all this happy work, the little cobbler could never find the time to make a new pair of shoes for himself.
"D'ye know," he'd often say to strangers, with a merry grin, "THE COBBLER'S ALWAYS THE WORST SHOD!"

Other titles in the Beaver/Sparrow Picture Book series:

An American Tail
The Bad Babies Counting Book Tony Bradman and Debbie van der Beek
Bear Goes to Town Anthony Browne
The Big Sneeze Ruth Brown
Crazy Charlie Ruth Brown
The Grizzly Revenge Ruth Brown
If At First You Do Not See Ruth Brown
Our Cat Flossie Ruth Brown
Harriet and William and the Terrible Creature Valerie Carey and Lynne Cherry
In the Attic Hiawyn Oram and Satoshi Kitamura
Ned and the Joybaloo Hiawyn Oram and Satoshi Kitamura
What's Inside? Satoshi Kitamura
The Adventures of King Rollo David McKee
The Further Adventures of King Rollo David McKee
The Hill and the Rock David McKee
I Hate My Teddy Bear David McKee
King Rollo's Letter and Other Stories David McKee
King Rollo's Playroom David McKee
Not Now Bernard David McKee
Two Can Toucan David McKee
Two Monsters David McKee
Tusk Tusk David McKee
The Truffle Hunter Inga Moore
The Vegetable Thieves Inga Moore
Babylon Jill Paton Walsh and Jennifer Northway
Robbery at Foxwood Cynthia and Brian Paterson
The Foxwood Treasure Cynthia and Brian Paterson
The Foxwood Regatta Cynthia and Brian Paterson
The Foxwood Kidnap Cynthia and Brian Paterson
The Tiger Who Lost His Stripes Anthony Paul and Michael Foreman
The Magic Pasta Pot Tomie de Paola
Mary Had a Little Lamb Tomie de Paola
We Can Say No! David Pithers and Sarah Greene
The Boy Who Cried Wolf Tony Ross
Goldilocks and the Three Bears Tony Ross
The Three Pigs Tony Ross
Terrible Tuesday Hazel Townson and Tony Ross
There's A Crocodile Under My Bed Dieter and Ingrid Schubert
Emergency Mouse Bernard Stone and Ralph Steadman
Inspector Mouse Bernard Stone and Ralph Steadman
Quasimodo Mouse Bernard Stone and Ralph Steadman
The Fox and the Cat Kevin Crossley-Holland and Susan Varley
Crocodile Teeth Marjorie Ann Watts
The Tale of Fearsome Fritz Jeanne Willis and Margaret Chamberlain
The Tale of Mucky Mabel Jeanne Willis and Margaret Chamberlain

PIASIER AZTECA SOU YEN GROSCHEN PAI STIVER
CENTIME FRANC CENT CENTAVO FRANC DOLLAR DRAC
AZTECA ANNA POUND ESCUDO SEN PENNY KOPECK BELGA
GUILDER KOPECK PIASTER SOL DO RIAL SOLDO SEN CONT
PESO SOU FRANC LIRA CONTO RUBLE RUPEE SOLDO CENT
RUBLE CONTO YEN PESETA SHEKEL BELGA
CONTO KRONA PIE DOLLAR REIS CENTAVO
ESCUDO GUILDER DRACHMA DINAR SCHILLING KOPECK ESCU
PESETA STIVER CONT
SEN BELGA KOPECK KRONA KRONA
KRONA KOPECK LIRA CENT PESO LIRA
CENTIME PAI DOLLAR LIRA KRONA CENTIMO FRANC RIAL CENT
SHEKEL PENNY CENT KRONE BELGA PFEN KRONE DUIT KRONE
CENTIMO PIASTER PIASTER ESCUDO SEN RUBLE
FRANC PESO SCHILLING MARK ESCUDO CENT
AZTECA BELGA CENTAVO RUPEE
FLORIN GULDEN CENTISIMO SHEKEL POUND DOL
PFENNIG SHEKEL SOU
SEN SOU CENTAVO CONTO KOPECK FRANS
REIS PIASTER DRACHMA SOLDO RUPEE POUND MARK
STIVER KRONA MARK STIVER POUND
CENTIME SEN PESO DINAR ANNA
MARK CENTIME RIAL CENT FLORIN
STIVER DOLLAR AZTECA YEN SEN
GROSCHEN CENTIMO
PESETA DRACHMA CENTISIMO SOLDO ANNA
BELGA RUPEE DINAR PESO SOU DINAR AZTECA CENTIM PESE
ALEX GROSCHEN
FRANC SEN RUPEE YEN FRANC RUBLE SCHILLING BELGA
PIASTER CONTO SEN DOLLAR LIRA POUND

SOLDO CENT DINAR MARK SCHILLING PAI DINAR REIS
AZTECA SHEKEL PIASTER GROSCHEN CENT DI YEN ANNA
YEN SOU ESCUDO CONTO MARK PENNY SCHILLING PFENNIG AZTECA RUBLE STIVER
FLORIN AZTECA SEN FLORIN SCHILLING
PAI ESCUDO CENT ANNA MARK BELGA
GUILDER YEN CENTESIMO DINAR SOU LIRA FRANC
RUBLE REIS BELGA SOU PESETA RUBLE PESETA ESCUDO
ANNA FRANC LIRA DRACHMA YEN SHEKEL
CENTAVO DRACHMA RUBLE KOPECK MARK GROSCHEN PIASTER RUBLE
SOLDO CONTO RUPEE RUPEE LIRA CENTAVO PENNY KRONA
ESCUDO ANNA REIS KOPECK SEN CONTO DRACHMA KOPECK SOU
SOU FLORIN CONTO STIVER CENTAVO PAI PESETA PIASTER
STIVER REIS CENTIMO PESO SCHILLING REIS STIVER GULDEN
LIRA CENTESIMO KRONA DOLLAR FRANC RIAL CENTIME DINAR
SOU PENNY PESO GUILDER POUND SHEKEL
PAI KRONE GUILDER GROSCHEN FLORIN FLORIN
SOU LIRA KRONA POUND CENTESIMO RUBLE
POUND KRONE SOLDO AZTECA PENNY DOLLAR
ANNA GROSCHEN CENTESIMO STIVER KOPECK
PESETA MARK GROSCHEN PESO FRANC SCHILLING
CENTESIMO SOU CENTAVO SHEKEL PESO
DUIT KOPECK KRONA REIS CENTIMO MARK AZTECA
SCHILLING FLORIN GROSHEN ESCUDO POUND FLORIN
PIASTER SOU KRONA DUIT CENT ANNA
ANNA GUILDER YEN
GROSCHEN YEN BELGA DRACHMA FRANC CONTO SHEKEL
KRONA MARK RUBLE ESCUDO RIAL DOLLAR
SHEKEL SEN POUND KOPECK
ESCUDO SOL RUBLE
PESETA LIRA PESETA PIE